MW00954209

Copyright © 2018 TJ Trumar

All rights reserved.

No part of this publication may be reproduced, distributed, or transmitted in any form or by any means, including photocopying, recording, or other electronic or mechanical methods, without the prior written permission of the publisher, except in the case of brief quotations embodied in reviews and certain other noncommercial uses permitted by copyright law.

The moral right of the author and illustrator has been asserted.

Cover design and illustrations by Patrick Marston

Hardback ISBN-13: 978-0-9600783-0-1

Paperback ISBN-13: 978-0-9600783-1-8

eBook ISBN-13: 978-0-9600783-2-5

Dedication

R, J & T, - For the years of fun stories! I am so thankful to call you mine.
For J, thank you for giving this dream a purpose and never giving up. - T

For Chris, who always supports me. For Diane, who always inspires me.
For Tabitha, who made my dream come true. - J

For my wife, Arielle. Thank you for her patience through late nights as I painted each page.
And for my scotties, Maisie and Miles, who inspired the look of the bearded dragons. - Patrick

Truett's Dreamtime Adventures

THE LOST DRAGON

By TJ Trumar

Illustrated by Patrick N. Marston

The further Truett walked into the woods, the louder the sound. *What could it be?*

Truett walked a little further and suddenly he saw it—a baby dragon!

The dragon cowered and trembled at the sight of Truett. His wings were soaked with his tears.

"I'm Joseph," the dragon sniffled through his tears. "What's your name?"

"My name is Truett.
Why are you crying, Joseph?"

"I am lost and can't find my mommy."

"That is so sad!"
Truett exclaimed.
"But maybe I can help!
I am good with directions."

"Really?" said Joseph. " I can fly pretty well, but I get distracted easily. Maybe if we work together I'll be able to get home! Just climb on my back. I can fly you above the trees so you'll be able to see everything!"

Truett crawled onto
Joseph's back.

They flew high
into the sky.

As they soared over the forest,
Truett smiled from ear to ear with amazement.
Everything is so cool up here! Truett thought.

"So, Joseph, does your mom look a lot like you?" Truett shouted over the sound of the wind.

Joseph, who loved to talk about his mommy, answered happily. "We have the same stripes! But she just has a lot more than I do because she is old. She is also very tall and gives the best hugs!"

Joseph and Truett kept looking, but had no luck.

Suddenly, Truett had an idea.

"Can you describe your home?" he asked Joseph.

As the dragon talked about where he lived, Truett's grin grew wider.

"I know exactly where that is! My daddy takes me around there all the time."

Joseph's ears perked up.
"That's great! Just tell me where
to go and hold on real tight!"

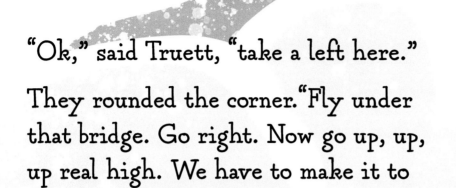

"Ok," said Truett, "take a left here."

They rounded the corner. "Fly under that bridge. Go right. Now go up, up, up real high. We have to make it to the top of that mountain up ahead."

When they got just over the edge of the mountain, Truett shouted, "I see her, I see her!"

Joseph began to fly in excited circles, forgetting about Truett hanging onto his back.

Truett's screams turned into roars of excitement.

Joseph flew as fast as he could toward his home and slid in for a landing.

His mommy
greeted him with
her wings wide
open, giving
Joseph the biggest
hug ever!

She hadn't noticed Truett yet,
so he received his first mommy-
dragon hug, too. She squeezed so
hard that Truett let out a squeak.

Joseph's mommy heard the noise.

"Oh, who's this?"

Joseph said, "This is my new friend, Truett. He helped me find my way home."

"Thank you so much for bringing my sweet boy back to me!" Joseph's mommy said, giving him a big, big hug. "I bet your mommy is getting worried about you. It's starting to get dark. Would you like me to fly you home?"

Truett said, "Would I like it? I would LOVE it!"

The mommy dragon gave Truett a very warm smile. "Great! Climb up, boys, and we will fly high with the stars on our way to your house!"

"OK!!!"

The ride home was even more
fun than the ride with Joseph
earlier. He could see lights
in the houses below and the
stars and moon above him.

Upon arriving at Truett's home, they found his mommy outside looking for him.

She greeted him with a huge hug. She thanked Joseph and his mommy for bringing her son home safely. Truett and his mommy waved goodbye as his new friends flew away.

Truett turned to his mommy and said, "BEST DAY EVER!"

The End

ABOUT THE AUTHORS

Tabitha gets the most joy from watching her children grow, explore and embrace the thrill of life. She and her husband love to travel, discover new things, and are huge foodies. It is Tabitha's hope that when she writes, it provokes thoughts and sparks the imagination of all readers. May this book and many others, provide hope to all the dreamers out there!

Jessica loves hanging out with her amazing husband. She spends most of her time reading, crocheting, writing and cuddling with her four dogs. She has loved reading since she was very young. She hopes that many children will call a TJ Trumar book their favorite.

ABOUT THE ILLUSTRATOR

Patrick N. Marston works as a graphic designer and freelance illustrator and lives in Little Rock, AR with his wife, Arielle and two scottish terriers.

Made in the USA
Lexington, KY
11 November 2019

56799140R00024